The New Adventures of the Little Red Hen

L. K. Merideth

For all the little chicks at Sycamore School.

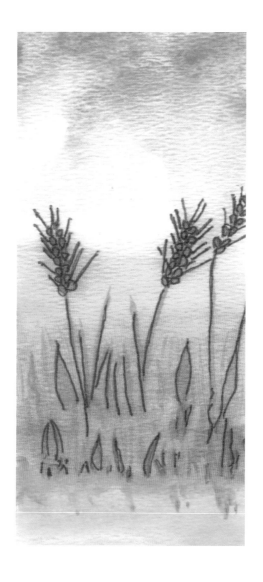

It is known far and wide,
So surely you know,
Of the time the Little Red Hen,
Put on a show.

She found a grain of wheat,
And with no help, it is so.
Created a tasty treat,
With her little chicks in tow.

Not one single animal
Would help her when asked.
But when time came for eating,
Well, the line it was vast!

While the moral was clear,
To my gentle reader here.
With the barnyard brigade,
Confusion yet reigns my dear.

Do you think they learned a lesson,
And helped so they could dine?
I am so sorry to report
These folks did not learn the first time.

Instead of pitching in,
And helping with the labor.
They sat amongst themselves,
Developing a plan to betray her.

While it would have been easy and fun to help with the tasks,
Wheat planting, tending, milling did not seem a blast.
The barnyard animals as lazy things will do,
Decided instead to throw a wrench in it too!
They spent their days not in their errors fixing,
With jealousy they raged in duplicity mixing.

Amongst themselves they planned,
There had to be some way.
To just waltz in for bread,
And with no labor pay.

Who was the first one to attack,
And give it a start?
Well what would you guess?
The beautiful goose played her part!

She thought herself quite lovely,
No scratching in the dirt for her!
Hard labor and exhaustion,
Well, no way, I'm sure!

As events would turn out,
The Red Hen made a name for herself.
Her fresh from the farm bread,
Became a hit unto itself.

Everything old becomes new again, sure.
The fresh food movement started,
And was quite the rage I have heard.
Suddenly everyone wanted a taste of the treat,
Lovingly tended on a farm,
From their very own wheat!

Word spread far and wide,
That it was transformed through great care,
Through every step of the process,
The Red Hen was a baker beyond compare.

Soon the time came for the Interstate Fair.
The goose was driven to distraction,
What if the hen were to earn renown there?

She just wouldn't have it!
Share the spotlight with a hen?
Who cares if she did the work?
Fame, fortune and praise were for the goose pen!

"I wouldn't mind having a blue ribbon or two,
Plotted the conceited old goose, since she'd no work to do.
That dumb old chicken won't be any the wiser it's true!
She can work. She can work. All the day through.
When it's time to compete,
And earn praise for her feat,
I'll fly in and present that taste tempting treat.

I'll be showered with prizes,
Fame and fortune too.
When you are as pretty as I,
These things are owed to you.

She had wanted my help.
So here, I am giving it too!
She should not complain.
It is one task less to do!"

So she set out to complete her plan with zeal,
She found likeminded friends to whom work was not part of the deal,
The promise of fame and fortune to them most appealed.
Sounded like a great plan, so her prize they would steal.

The plump little pig,
Was still bent out of shape.
She could not believe it,
When she was handed her fate.

Said the goose to the pig, "look, here is the plan.
Keep a piggy-eye on the hen that is all I demand.
Mark all her tasks. Take note of her work.
When it's time to compete.
When her work is complete,
We'll waltz before the judges,
With our answers replete."

We'll know just what to say,
About our work all the day.
But not one backache or nail-break,
Will we endure in our way!

Well back at the hen house,
The Little Red Hen was not bothered.
Without fair-weather friends,
She was closer to the victory started!

Why should she provide them with bread?
What would be expected of her next?
It just filled her with dread.
Well, who needs them when there is work to be done?
She could find real friends instead,
Who thought work was fun.

The old farmer's dog
Was a smart one, between me and you!
And oh my goodness me,
He could dig it was true!

When it was time to plant the wheat,
It was as if it was no work to do.
The happy dog would quickly,
Dig up the earth for you!

Once having made flour from wheat,
They made a discovery too!
There is no limit to the treats and things now in your view!
So many sweet things, so much work to do,
So many possibilities to ponder for you.

Then from the forest some animals came.
Not having to toil and work in the rain?
Well to this wild crew that sounded insane!
And they would be rewarded with baked goods?
Well who could complain?

The squirrels brought walnuts to bake into pie.
A bear with a sweet-tooth ventured in with some honey to try.
They made delicious buns, muffins and cakes,
To enjoy with some tea, during their breaks.

When it came time to plant the wheat,
Well it was hard to compete,
With the nimble squirrels,
And their tiny feet.

When cutting and threshing time came for the wheat,
The strong arms of the bear,
Made this job an easy feat!

Up with the sun, till the workday was done.
Home again, home again, their words often spun.
Of memories and planning of the work yet to come.
How hard it had been, how nice it would be.
Perhaps they would try something new, wait and see.

The plump little pig spent the day wallowing away.
The goose spent her time preening to look fab on the day.
She practiced her schmoozing and the speech she would say,
When she would pick-up the prizes for the bread one day.

Well don't worry dear reader,
There is no cause to fret.
The chicken was not dumb,
Nor were the friends she had met!

Soon it was time for the Interstate Fair.
The lazy farm animals would make their fame there!

The goose was ready to hatch her fabulous plan.
She had a new hat to wear! She was poised and fair!
The pig would stay behind that curtain there.
She would pretend she was a hard working hen that was scared,
To come out on stage, she was too meek and too mild.
She was just happy to work away with a smile.

And so it began,
The goose took to the stage.
She bantered and strutted and showed her long legs.
The judges draped in darkness were seated off stage.
They asked pointed questions about the loaf that was made.

When questions were asked of the marvelous crew,
The plump little pig whispered about just what to do.
The goose repeated the tale,
Of the toil and labor you must do,
Through each and every season,
To create this delicacy for you.

She detailed her hard work, and that of the farm animals too!
The goose blushed and batted her eyes. She was so shy, it is true!
She repeated after the pig, had the judges in her hand she knew.
Not afraid of hard work, it was the right thing to do!

After the presentation, direct from *Paris*.
The announcer came out to direct the jury!

"Now you have tasted this fab-u-lous bread,
Shall we hear from the judges,
What thoughts they have in their head?!

We have assembled for this task,
Judges with whom few can compete.
Direct from the World's Fair in France,
We have tasters, *magnifique*!

First in their class
They have world renown, no?
They have won best bread,
In *Paris*, you know?

It is my great honor to introduce to you now,
The panel of judges who will decide your fate, and how.
First and foremost we have the farmer's old dog,
The squirrels you know, from their fabulous job.
One large brown bear with a delicate palate,
And baker *extraordonaire*, Little Red Hen.
There you have it!

Now just before I turn it over to them,
Let me tell you now about the fabulous prizes you win!
A prize it is sure, for which all bakers would fight,
To work for the Red Hen and her crew day and night!"

Suddenly, off to stage right,
The sound of thundering pig hooves gave all quite a fright!
They tore down the curtain as they thundered away,
One fat little pig and a goose leading the way!

"Wait! Stop!" said the hen and her wonderful crew!
"I think you have won, and there is much work to do!
How fantastic it is that you enjoy labor too!
We had no idea, but we can't wait for you!"

Well the pig and the goose, they knew they were through.
No way would they accept a fate of work, not these two.
So that was the last we have seen of them,
Heading off into the night, our fair-weather friends.

A disgraced lazy pig and the vindictive goose,
As far as we know they are still on the loose.
So if you are planning an enterprise beyond compare,
I would suggest you be wary if you see these two there!

The Red Hen and her crew,
Were back on the farm as they would do.
To sing, and to bake and to farm the day through!
Yes they work hard, and have some backaches,
But there is no other reward in the world they would take!

So on each morning, when you see the sun break,
You can choose to take pride in the work that you make.
Whatever it may be or what form it takes,
However hard you toil, or how your heart aches.
You can always be judged by your good works in time,
Be true to yourself and you'll win and be fine.
For no one can ever take that away,
When you've done a good job,
And made the most of the day.

Made in the USA
San Bernardino, CA
12 September 2014